Published and distributed by:

ISLAND HERITAGE
P U B L I S H I N G

99-880 IWAENA STREET, AIEA, HAWAII 96701-3202
PHONE: (808) 487-7299 • FAX: (808) 488-2279
EMAIL: hawaii4u@pixi.com

ISBN#: 0-89610-351-X

First Edition, First Printing - 1998

AUNTIE

Story by Stephany Indie . Illustrations by Diane Kraul

In memory of Stephany,
friend and storyteller

and for Maile and Michael

Aloha nui loa.

♥

Auntie wanted a new muʻumuʻu. She went to (Ala Moana) Shopping
Center and found the perfect fabric to make herself a muʻumuʻu.

Auntie went home, laid out the fabric, cut out the pieces, stitched them up, and put on the most beautiful mu'umu'u you ever saw.

She wore her elegant muʻumuʻu when she went to Kawaiahaʻo Church

and when she danced the hula.

She wore it and wore it and wore it and wore it. One day Auntie took her muʻumuʻu out of the closet and said, "Aiiiiiiii, it's faded!"

Very carefully Auntie took the muʻumuʻu all apart, cut out the
faded pieces and discovered she had just enough to make. . .

a handsome shirt.

Auntie wore her shirt when she went to watch the
outrigger canoe races at Kailua Beach.

Kanaha

She wore that shirt when she went shopping in Chinatown.
She wore it and wore it and wore it.

One day Auntie took her shirt out of the closet
and said, "Aiiiiiiii, it's faded!"

Auntie took the shirt all apart and cut out the faded pieces.
She discovered she had just enough to make...

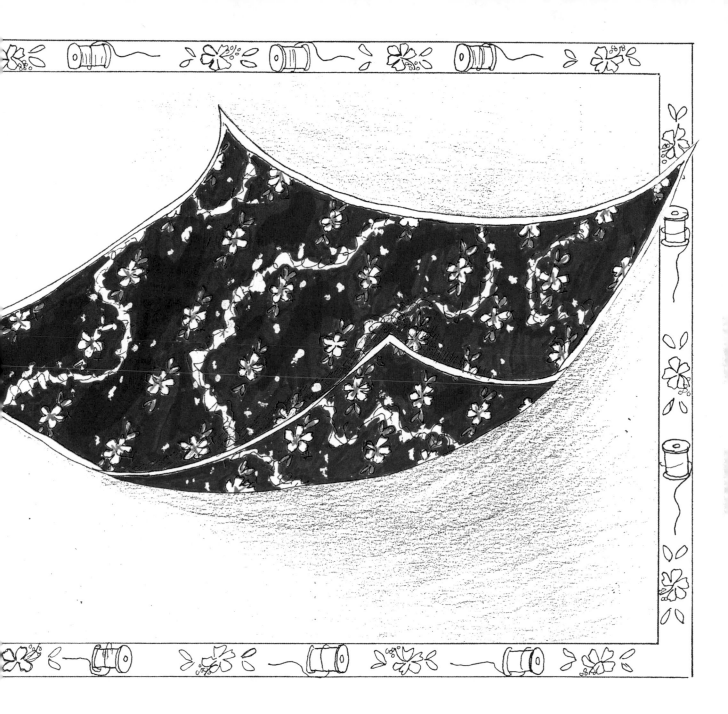

a scarf.

Auntie wore that scarf around her neck with flowers.

Sometimes when the gentle rains fell,
Auntie tied the scarf around her hair.

Auntie wore that scarf and wore it and wore it. One day she took it
out of her closet, looked at the scarf and said, "Aiiiiiiii, it's faded!"

Auntie laid out the scarf, cut out the faded parts
and had just enough to make...

a hat band for her lau hala hat.

Auntie wore her hat to the Kamehameha Day Parade in Lahaina

and she wore that hat when she "talked story" with her friends.

Auntie wore that hat and wore it and wore it. One day she took her
hat off, looked at the hat band and said, "Aiiiiiiii, it's faded!

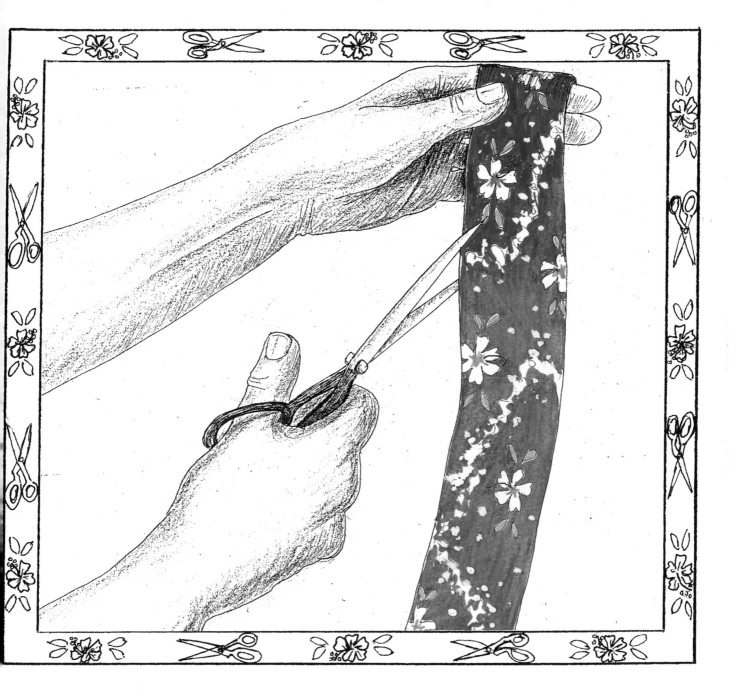

Auntie laid out the hat band, cut out the faded
parts and had just enough to make . . .

a pair of button earrings.

Auntie wore those earrings everywhere. She liked the feel of the
fabric so much that she would rub the earrings.
Finally, even the earrings wore out.

And so, of the beautiful mu'umu'u, the handsome shirt,
the scarf, the hat band and the earrings

Auntie has nothing left . . . except

the story you just read

and the memories. ALL PAU!

- NOTES -

Aiiiiiiii An expression used in a time of distress, common to the Hawaiian language.

Auntie An affectionate title given to women relatives or women greatly respected in Hawai'i.

Chinatown An old section of Honolulu. Markets there are still owned and operated by the Chinese. Many wonderful herbs, teas, and Chinese delicacies can be purchased there.

Kamehameha Day Parade Held every June to honor King Kamehameha, who united the Hawaiian Islands under one rule.

Kailua Beach Located on the windward side of O'ahu. This is the favorite beach of the author and her children.

Kawaiaha'o Church Located in Honolulu. It is the first church the missionaries built on O'ahu in the 1800's. At one time the royalty attended this church. Today at certain services, prayers, sermons and hymns can still be heard spoken in the Hawaiian language.

Lau hala The leaf of the pandanas tree. Used by the Hawaiians to weave hats, fans, clothing items and mats.

Mu'umu'u A long dress usually made of cotton, worn in Hawai'i. This dress was introduced by the missionaries. Today the mu'umu'u can be plain and worn almost anywhere, or it can be fancy and worn to parties. Elegant dresses like the mu'umu'u, called the holokū, are often worn as wedding dresses.

Outrigger canoe races Once a sport enjoyed only by the royalty in Hawai'i. Paddling, as it is called locally, is now enjoyed by everyone and is a very competitive sport. Some of the canoes are carved from koa wood and are very special.

"Talk story" An island expression for getting together and discussing the news or gossiping.